Energy IN SPORT

Nicolas Brasch

Australia • Brazil • Japan • Korea • Mexico • Singapore • Spain • United Kingdom • United States

Energy in Sports

Fast Forward
Green Level 13

Text: Nicolas Brasch
Editor: Kate McGough
Designer: Stella Vassiliou
Series Designer: James Lowe
Production Controller: Emma Hayes
Photo Research: Corrina Tauschke
Audio recordings: Juliet Hill, Picture Start

Speakers: Matthew King and Abbe Holmes

Acknowledgements
The author and publisher would like to acknowledge permission to reproduce material from the following sources: Photographs by AAP Image, pp. 5 bottom left, 6, 7, 8, 13, 16, 17/ Franck Fife, p. 18; Alamy Images/Grant Pritchard, p. 10; Getty Images, p. 23/ Fat Chance Productions, p. 11/ Andy Lyons, p. 21/ Clive Mason, p. 19; Newsphotos.com, pp. 3, 4, 5 top left, 15; AFP/Fabrice Cofftini, cover, p. 1, 9; Photolibrary.com/Jenny Mills, p. 22/ Rosenfeld, p. 14.

ISBN 978 0 17 012582 6
ISBN 978 0 17 012573 4 (set)

Cengage Learning Australia
Level 7, 80 Dorcas Street
South Melbourne, Victoria Australia 3205
Phone: 1300 790 853

Cengage Learning New Zealand
Unit 4B Rosedale Office Park
331 Rosedale Road, Albany, North Shore NZ 0632
Phone: 0800 449 725

For learning solutions, visit **cengage.com.au**

Printed in Australia by Ligare Pty Ltd
6 7 8 9 10 11 12 20 19 18 17 16

THE UNIVERSITY OF MELBOURNE

Evaluated in independent research by staff from the Department of Language, Literacy and Arts Education at the University of Melbourne.

Energy in Sport

Nicolas Brasch

Contents

Chapter 1

ENERGY IN SPORT

People who play sport need a lot of **energy**.
If they don't have energy,
they are not able to play at their **peak** for very long.

Sandy Blythe of Australia

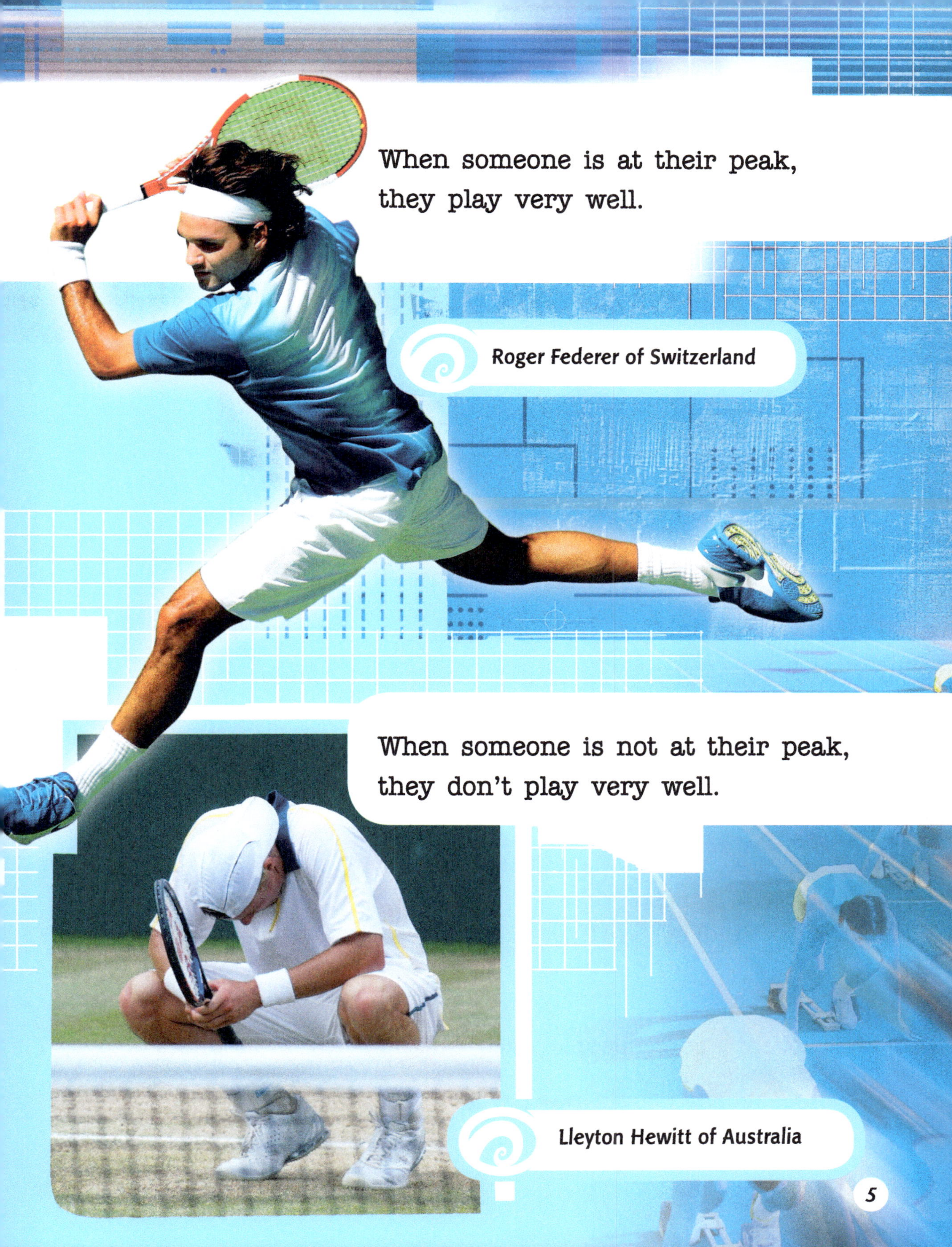

When someone is at their peak, they play very well.

Roger Federer of Switzerland

When someone is not at their peak, they don't play very well.

Lleyton Hewitt of Australia

Marlene Ottey,
sprinter from Jamaica

Different sports people need different kinds of energy.

Some sports people need a lot of energy quickly.
This is called an energy rush.

Other sports people need energy slowly over a long time.

Mizuki Noguchi,
endurance runner from Japan

Chapter 2

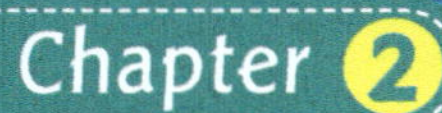

HOW SPRINTERS PREPARE

Sprinters are people who race over a short distance.

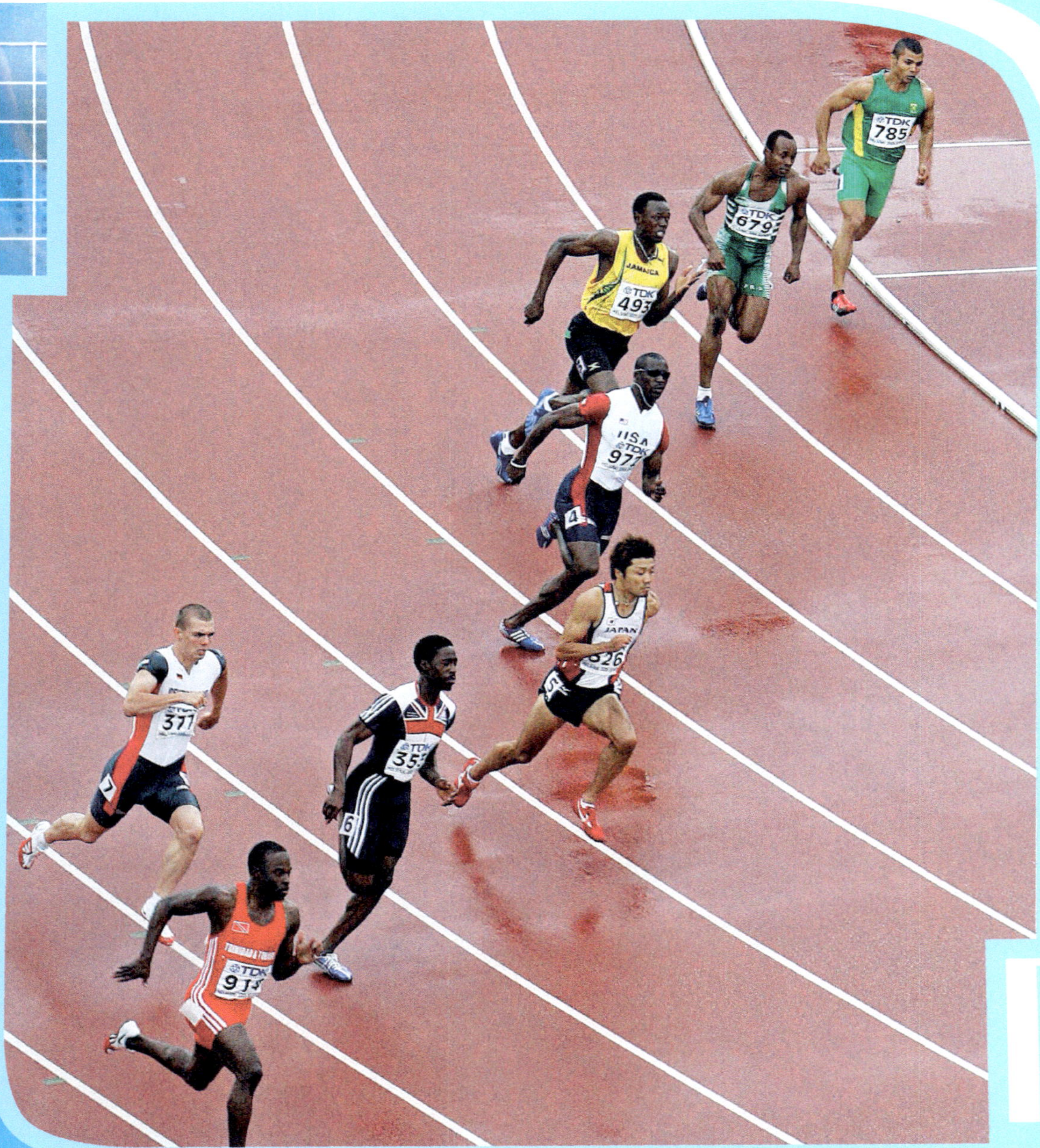

Sprinters need to build up speed very quickly. They need to have a lot of energy for a short time.

At the Olympic Games, there are three sprint races: the 100 metres, the 200 metres and the 400 metres.

Sprinters prepare for a race by building up their **muscles**. The stronger their muscles are, the more energy they can use at the start of a race.

Running Words 156

If a sprinter does not get a good start to his or her race, he or she will not keep up with the other sprinters.

Chapter 3

WHAT SPRINTERS EAT

Sprinters need special food to help them build their muscles.
The best foods for building muscles are foods with lots of **protein**.

foods with lots of protein

Proteins help bodies to grow.
They are also good for fixing **injured** bodies.
When sprinters injure their bodies,
they have to eat lots of foods with protein in them.

Protein can be found in red meat, eggs and milk.

A sprinter can eat eggs for breakfast every day. He or she can also have two serves of red meat and drink five glasses of milk every day.

Matt Shirvington of Australia

Chapter 4

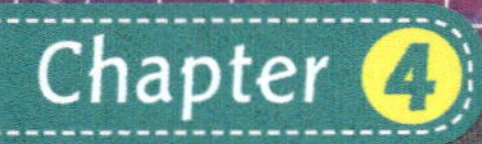

HOW ENDURANCE RUNNERS PREPARE

Endurance runners race over a long distance.

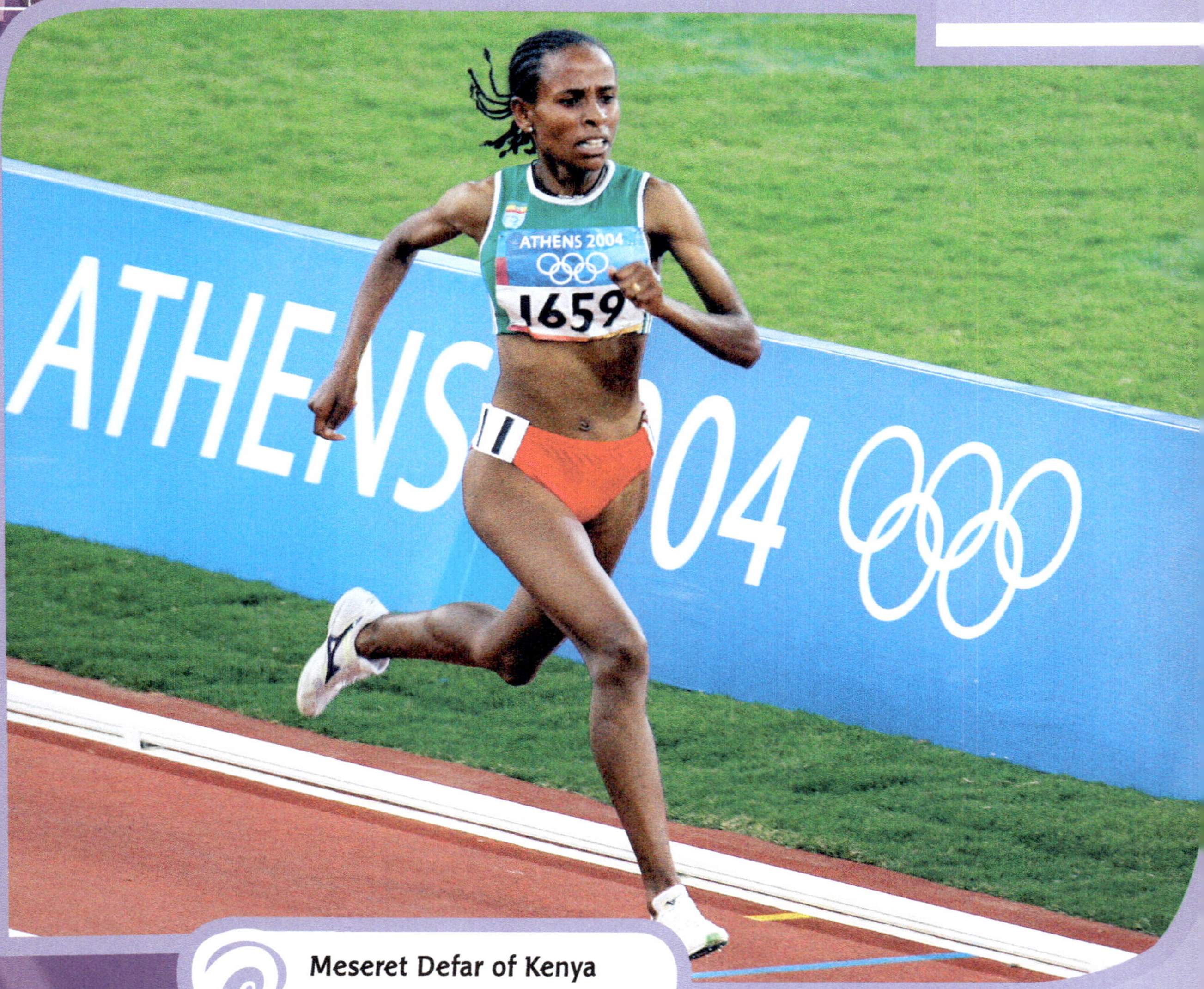

Meseret Defar of Kenya

At the Olympic Games, the endurance races are the 5000 metres, the 10 000 metres and the marathon. The marathon is run over 42 kilometres.

Kenenisa Bekele of Ethiopia

Endurance runners don't have big muscles like sprinters.

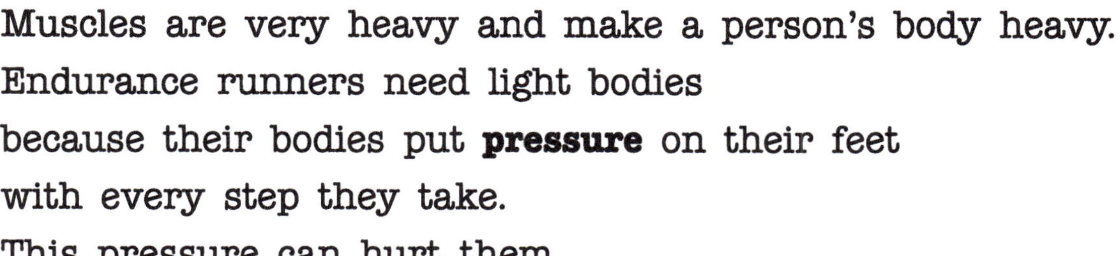

Muscles are very heavy and make a person's body heavy. Endurance runners need light bodies because their bodies put **pressure** on their feet with every step they take. This pressure can hurt them.

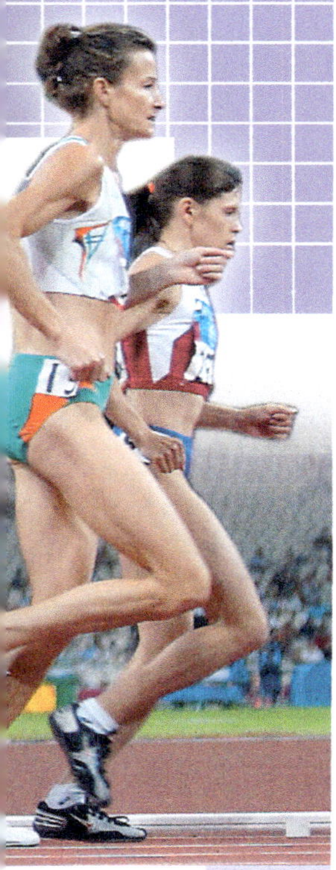

Lee Troop of Australia

Chapter 5

WHAT ENDURANCE RUNNERS EAT

Endurance runners need food that will give them the energy to keep running for a long time. The best kinds of foods for endurance runners are foods with lots of **carbohydrates** and **fat**.

foods high in fats or carbohydrates

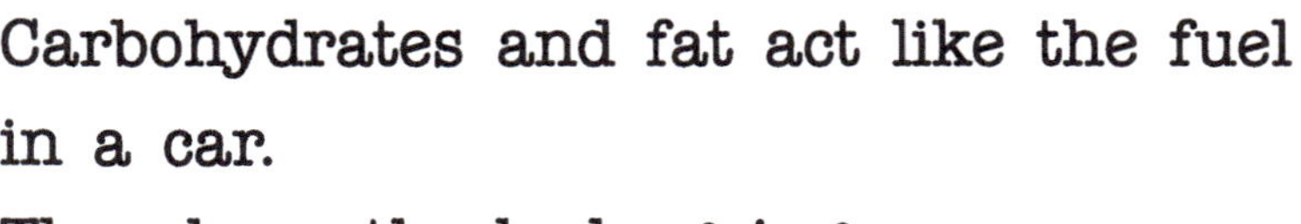

Carbohydrates and fat act like the fuel
in a car.
They keep the body going.

Sonia O'Sullivan of Ireland

Foods like pasta and cereals have lots of carbohydrates.
Carbohydrates can also be found in fruit and vegetables.
Fat can be found in butter and oil.

Endurance runners can eat cereal for breakfast, pasta for lunch and pasta for dinner.
This will give them the energy to run a long distance.

Paula Radcliffe of Great Britain

Glossary

carbohydrates sugars and starches that give energy to the body

energy the power to move

fat an oily substance that provides a lot of energy

injured hurt or damaged

muscles tissues in the body that allow us to move

peak the very best a person can play

pressure pushing hard on something

protein a nutrient that helps build many parts of the body

Index